GETTING IN

(How one ingenious applicant induced
a letter of acceptance from America's
most selective university)

by
Julian F. Thompson

Library of Congress Control Number 2009903691

ISBN 978-0-615-29047-8

For Rafer and Princess, and for Polly,
whose love radiates around us all

Tapioca Strangeways

P.O. Box 138
Rising Gorge, VT

Admissions Office
Riddle University
Riddle, MA

Dear Whatever Admissions Person Reads This,

As you know, applicants to Riddle are required to write an essay on the following topic:

> Referring specifically to the education you received in high school, answer the question "So what?" Confine your answer to a single page.

When I read that little sweetheart of a topic, I felt, with Samuel Beckett, that I had "nothing to express, nothing with which to express, nothing from which to express, no desire to express, together with an obligation to express."

So I had a problem.

But then I thought: How about if instead of writing my Essay on *your* topic I just cut some slices off of me and served them to you raw, unsauced, except for parts improved by my imagination?

Be warned, I'll need a whole lot more than just a single page, and I'd prefer to submit in chunks, over a few weeks time. Also: reader discretion is required.

What think you, O Gatekeeper to my Future Happiness?

Yours absolutely truly,

Tapioca Strangeways

Photo (of me) enclosed.

RIDDLE UNIVERSITY

Office of Admissions   Riddle University   Riddle, MA

Tapioca Strangeways
P.O. Box 138
Rising Gorge, VT

Dear Tapioca,

You've got an unusual name (nothing the matter with that!) that sort of goes with your unusual request (to do your Essay on a different topic than the one assigned). It landed on my desk and (I have to tell you) put back a light into my red-rimmed eyes. By suggesting it might pull some very different freight, you've moved (at least for me) the Admissions locomotive onto an exciting new track. In my experience, "So what?" turned out to be a question many applicants provided answers to that the FDA (and certainly S. Beckett) would deem unsuitable for human consumption.

So, by all means Do Your Thing. Being a bit younger and more "with it" than a number of my colleagues in Admissions (including our Director, Dr. Gladstone Bragg), and so in ways more influential in decision-making as well, I'll be able to give however many pages you submit a totally open-minded, discreetful, and respected reading. Feel free to "tell it like it is" and present yourself "unsauced" (as you so attractively put it). You're not going to "freak out" this admissions ossifer (misspelling intentional).

Interestedly,

Dean Dorman

PS You should know I'm not a Dean. Dean is my first name. Feel free to use it, writing me.

PPS And because not everything in this letter is exactly kosher (we have many chicken-s rules about the expression of personal opinions and so on, so forth), I think it best that you submit to me here at my home address (to which I've removed your folder). It's 1134 Honeysuckle Ct., South Riddle, MA.

PPPS Thanx for the photo. I can almost guarantee you your looks won't do damage to your application. Riddle doesn't discriminate on the basis of . . . . anything!

"Go Sphinxes"

Tapioca Strangeways

Dear Dean,

Okay – you *do* sound cool!   Your letter was unbelievable – awesome!   So, here are my first three chapters, and others should come soon.   Have a happy reading.   And by all means call me

Tapi

My Admissions Essay

Chapters 1,2,3

My Admissions Essay - Chapter 1

<u>The Genesis of my Application (?)</u>

I believe the first sounds I ever heard -
which would have made no sense at the time
- might have been the following:

<u>Enthusiastic Female Voice</u>   (my mother'd
opted for a midwife): "It's a . . . . .!"

<u>Male Voice</u> (according to legend, my
father's) interrupting: "I'll get a
preliminary Riddle application in the mail
toot sweet. For - let's see - the class of
two-oh-one-three, wouldn't that be about
right? Honey? Check my math, will you?
Wouldn't the little bugger matriculate in

the class of two thousand thirteen? At

Riddle?"

<u>Different, Exhausted-Sounding Female Voice</u>

(that would be my mother's): "What? I

guess . . . . Whatever. Are you sure the

little bugger's meant to be this color?"

Whether my father ever did get a
"preliminary application in the mail" way
back then or not, I don't know. But I
doubt it makes much difference either way,
I can't really imagine Riddle stamping
"Accepted" on the application, by proxy, of
a one-day old. TS

My Admissions Essay — Chapter 2

<u>Some Very Early Childhood Recollections</u>

The hospital I was born in was more gentrified, not to mention cleaner, than the building my mother and I joined my father in, after she was discharged. Yep, when I was little, we lived in the Projects on the 5th floor of a high-rise whose top floor was the 14th, one up from the 12th, because nobody in the building was crazy enough to live on 13.

If the elevator was out of order — and that happened a lot — we had to go up and down the stairs, which smelled of urine. One day, I ran into the person responsible for that smell, a man who was standing pissing on the staircase near the 4th floor doorway.

"How come you're doing that?" I asked him. "Don't you have a bathroom at home?"

"'Course I do." he said. "You think I like getting my shoes splattered off these steps, here? Head of the Tenants Association pays me; landlord can't raise the rents 'long as this stairway stinks, he thinks. I piss on odd-numbered floors Monday, Wednesday, and Friday, and even-numbered floors on Tuesday, Thursday, and Saturday. Seein' as this is Thursday, I'm watering number 4. Sundays, I keep my dick

in my pants and sit in the sweet-smellin'
house of the Lord."

Some days, I'd see people running up and
down the stairs after other people, often
hollering some form of the same word –
"mother" stuck in front of it, sometimes –
a word my father said couldn't be printed
in the *New York Times* and was not to be
used, ever, by kids my age.

As a rule, I'd squeeze over to one side and
let those people pass, but this one day I
asked a man, who had a pistol in his hand,
just exactly what he was doing.

He said "I'm on my way to give a man a
Smith-and-Wesson-oscopy," and he kept on

going.

I asked my father what that was and he explained it was a painful procedure not approved by the AMA, and I ought to stop speaking to strangers.

Although I'm pretty sure I never met a Riddle grad when we were living in the projects – other than my father whose claim to be one may be bogus – the things I experienced in and around our building – example above – I can now see as being part and parcel of a "liberal education."

When I was old enough to go to school, Dad said it was important for me to see "how the other half lives", so we moved into a beachfront home on Long Island, where I

continued to "prep" for Riddle.

My Admissions Essay – Chapter 3

<u>Meeting "the other half"</u>

The first members of "the other half" I remember meeting were Dorothy Pilchard, who was called "Dottie", and Miss Albright, who I assumed was her paid keeper, and was called "Miss Albright".

They were sitting side by side on the beach out in front of the Misabasquet Beach Club, where my father'd left me off. Smiling, I'd put my towel down on the sand near where they'd put their towels down and were sitting on them. In my mind, I was trying to be friendly.

"Dottie" – whose name I didn't know yet –

looked over at me, frowned, and said, "This
is a private beach, you know."

To which I replied, "I thought it belonged
to the Misabasquet Beach Club."

"That's what makes it private," Dottie
said. "So not just anybody can come and
sit on it."

"Well, I'm not just anybody," I told her.

"Oh, really?" she said. "I'm Dottie
Pilchard and I've never seen you before.
What's your name, anyway?"

I'd already gotten to dislike that tone of

voice of hers. It dripped with negativity, some of which splashed onto me and stung. I decided she didn't *deserve* to be told the truth, which made what I was going to do different from lying.

"Bronson Beaudabee," I announced, putting together the names of two of my father's dogs.

"That's a stupid name," she said. But I could tell from the look in her eye that she was not as sure of herself as she had been.

"So *you* say," I threw back at her, underlining my advantage with a little laugh. "I bet you've never even met a member of the Maltese royal family before."

That rocked chubby Dottie back on her fat little a-double-q. She turned to her companion for help.

"Someone who's what this person claims to be can't be a member of this club, can they Miss Albright?" she asked her.

Miss Albright now had a smear of uncertainty on her face, too. I figured she was trying to remember if she'd ever heard the word "Maltese" back in Limeyland, and if she had, whether it had had "royal family" after it, as in "a palace spokesman announced that the Queen had the Maltese royal family over for lunch on Tuesday."

I, of course, had only previously heard

"Maltese" with "terrier" after it, that

being what Bronson was, and Beaudabee.

"Let's toddle off now, ducks," said Miss A,

getting to her feet and passing on Dottie's

question. "Mummy said we should be bathed

and in our jammies by the time your Daddy's

home."

"Your *jammies*?" I cried, and this time I

whooped with laughter. Dottie had gotten

up and turned her back on me.

"Not your *jellies*, Dottie? Are you sure?"

I was smelling blood, so for good measure I

dredged up a line I'd heard on the stairway

in the Projects.

"It must be jelly 'cause jam don't shake like that!" I said, pointing at the Pilchard rear end.

She spun around and faced me.

"My Daddy's friends with the President, and our house is nicer than any old palace, I bet," was what she found in her comeback closet.

"Well, goody-guts for you-hoo!" I yelled after her. She'd turned and started towards the parking lot, leaving the towels and sandals for Miss Albright to pick up.

Mine was a pretty lame line, I know. I should have dug deeper, done better, but I was feeling a little guilty for claiming to

be royalty, when she had a connection to

the President. Even at age 6, or whatever

I was, I was a small "d" democrat.

Tapioca Strangeways

P.O. Box 138
Rising Gorge, VT

Dear Dean,

It wasn't like I was holding my breath waiting to hear from you about my first three Chapters. Believe me, I wasn't even counting on a "thank-you" note, like I was Granny and my Chapters were an itchy wool scarf I'd knitted you for Christmas.

But I must admit that right now I'm sitting here wondering if maybe my request to sort of "tell it like it is" - or "was" - wasn't an invasion-of-Iraq-sized mistake. Maybe I never should have started babbling on about myself. For all I know, every time a new slice of me slides through the mail slot of your front door and lands there on the rug, you look at it and go "What makes you think your life's so fascinating, Tapioca Strangeways?"

Have you, in other words, regretted the favor that you did me?

Tell me the truth, I can take it.

Fingers crossed, et cetera,

                         Tapi

PS Whatever. Here are two more "slices."

My Admissions Essay

Chapters 4,5

My Admissions Essay – Chapter 4

<u>My First Educational Decision</u>

At the time we arrived on Long Island – it was early August – my formal education hadn't begun, and it became the basis of a discussion – or debate, some would say a fight – my parents had while sitting at the kitchen table.

"I think I'd like to home-school Tapioca," my mother said; that was the kick-off. She'd also been the driving force behind my unusual first name. The year before, she'd explained to me she'd decided on it before I was born and that it didn't matter if I turned out to be a boy or a girl: she was going to name her baby after something she

really loved. My father then chimed in –
he'd been listening – with "You could've
chosen Cecil or Cecilia." But for whatever
reason she didn't comment on his comment.

Now they were sitting opposite each other,
both with teaspoons in their hands.
Between them on the table was a much
diminished bowl of cherries jubilee that
they were now able to start on. It had
long since flamed out, many of the brandy-
soaked cherries had been eaten, and the
vanilla ice cream under them had gotten
awfully soupy.

There was a small TV high on a shelf behind
my mother, and the show on it, as I
recall, was Law and Order Criminal Intent.

My dad was looking up at it as he ate.

"I want our kid to have a good solid foundation in the basics," my mother continued. She picked up one of the cherries between her right thumb and forefinger and threw it at my father, hitting him on the forehead, right above the start of his nose.

"You hearing what I'm saying, Cecil?" she wanted to know.

"Of course I am," he said. "I can do two things at once — as you well know. But school is where a kid can learn the basics best." He picked the cherry off the front of his shirt and aimed it at my mother's heart.

"So, there," he added.

I was perched on one of the kitchen
counters in my p.j.s, listening. I'd
already brushed my teeth, which is why I
hadn't tried to get in on the snacking. If
I had, my mother would have made me brush
again and probably floss, too. Then and
now, I'm no big fan of flossing. So from
where I was I just watched my mother catch
that cherry before it hit her, and then put
it back where she'd gotten it from in the
first place. It seemed she'd opted for
diplomacy rather than war.

"Kids learn reading best sitting on their

mother's lap," she said soothingly. "And I can teach a child to do basic arithmetic the old-fashioned way, with pencil and paper, and prove her answers are correct, instead of putting faith in a calculator some wiseguy over in China could have trained to lie! In a classroom, there's a bunch of other kids jackassing around and wasting everybody's time. At home, a child can get things done, Cece."

"Kids need to be with other kids," my father countered. "They need the competition, to be part of the mainstream."

"Phooey," said my mom. "The mainstream's full of folks who aren't smart enough to realize what's up with the environment, who like their cars big and their movies

bloody, and who'll vote for whoever's said

the loudest that they're the ones who're

going to keep them safe."

"Maybe we should just ask Tapioca," said my

dad. "To choose between playing with other

boys and girls all day, or being stuck at

home with Mommy dear."

He gave the last two words the ring of

"child molester."

They both turned their heads to look at me.

I examined the alternatives. On the one

hand, being safely in a room containing a

refrigerator that was bursting with treats

like leftover cherries jubilee, or, on the other, swimming with a school of Dottie Pilchards.

My father was smiling at me, looking confident. My mother was smiling too, but she was also scooping up a big spoonful of soft vanilla ice cream with a cherry on top of it, and pointing it not toward herself but at me.

It was a classic no-brainer. "I choose home-school," I announced. I was cool enough not to jump off the counter and collect my bribe, and my mother was cool enough to give it a U-turn and pop it into her own mouth before my father turned back toward her.

I knew she would reward me in due time, but more importantly I also derived from this experience a wonderful sense of being capable of making my own educational decisions – the most recent of which is behind this application.

I tell you that just in case you are thinking for a minute I'm applying now because my father wants me to. To tell you the truth, I'm still a little pissed at him for presuming to apply *for* me, if he did, seventeen years ago, before I was capable of making *any* decisions, including whether or not to roll over.

My Admissions Essay - Chapter 5

<u>Serious Music and Me</u>

I suppose my mother should get credit for serious music being so much a part of my life. Yes, music and spirituality, too, as a matter of fact. I was introduced to both during my fifth year of home-schooling, which also happened to be the year I learned all about snakes in our Science unit.

What Mom did to kick off the music thing was to homemake some little frozen Popsicles - my favorite flavor: cherry - using oboe reeds as sticks and giving me a quarter for every five minutes I kept one of those reeds, stripped of its frozen

coating, in my mouth which would, she said,
"condition" it. That made no sense to me,
at first.

Actually, I'm much more into cooperation
and the barter system, but to the extent
that I have competitive juices and a love
of money, her offer got those two awake and
flowing - or whatever. And whenever I was
sitting around sucking, with a stopwatch
keeping track of my earnings, she used that
time to tell me what a great instrument the
oboe is.

When she casually added that it's sometimes
called the "clown prince of the orchestra",
I knew I had to have one. You see, my
parents watched a "Seinfeld" re-run and/or

"The Daily Show" with Jon Stewart almost every afternoon or evening, and my smart Mom knew that being a comic headliner on the tube was, at that time, one of my ambitions. It no longer is, though since then I've realized that having a sense of humor is a mental health necessity, given this crazy time in history we're living in.

My mother had little trouble locating an oboe on eBay, but finding me a teacher way out there on Long Island was more of a problem. The person she finally unearthed wasn't primarily "an oboe player." Mom met him when she went looking for a Science teacher/herpetologist who could teach her to teach me about snakes. But at one of their Science meetings, he admitted that he "fooled around on the oboe." That was enough for Mom; she'd found my oboe instructor.

In fact, as it turned out, and as far as I was ever able to tell, his "fooling around" had resulted only in his being able to play, perfectly, over and over, one little fragment of music. He told my mother that once I, too, mastered it, I would then be able to play "anything in the oboe repertory." The hard part of oboeing, he said, was coming to grips with the "personality" of the oboe reed.

You're probably familiar with the melody he set out to teach me to play. It's the one kids sing when they put a certain sentence to music.

The sentence? It's this, or something close to this: "No, they don't wear pants in the southern part of France."

If you're not familiar, ask around. A lot of people know it.

The original name of this Science teacher/ herpetologist/oboe/instructor was Roland Boyle, but he was in the process of legally changing it to Dhat Yurka. Mom said she wasn't sure what he wanted me to call him.

Well, he made that clear as soon as he walked into our kitchen, where I awaited him.

"Hello, Tapioca," he said to me. He was a tall young man with a blond mustache who was wearing a light blue turban. "My name is Dhat Yurka. D-H-A-T, Y-U-R-K-A. You can call me Dhat."

"The 'h' in Dhat is silent," my mother told me, trying to be helpful.

"Not if you say the name *right*," the man contradicted her, emphatically.

"So, Dhat . . . .," I started.

"Pardon?" he said, interrupting, with his eyebrows raised and looking cross. I guess I must have mispronounced the 'h'.

"D*hat* . . .?" I tried again, not exactly *saying* the 'h', but not ignoring it, either.

"Yes?" he answered, nodding and smiling.

"How come you've got that funny hat on?" I wanted to know.

"It's not a 'funny hat'," he told me, gently. "It's called a turban. I wear it because I'm thinking that I want to be a Sikh man."

What I heard, of course, was "sick man." "You *want* to get sick?" I blurted out. "Why? I *hate* getting sick."

"Not *sick*," he told me. "Sikh. S-I-K-H.

There's an enunciated 'h' at the end. Sort

of like the one in Dhat. *Sikh*," he said

again. It still sounded like "sick" to me.

"I've been studying this religion called

Sikhism," he went on. "It's big-time,

number five in the world with over twenty

million followers. I'll tell you more

about it later. But first, let's get our

oboes out and start tootling."

And that's what we did. I quickly

discovered that coaxing any purely musical

sound out of *my* oboe took a lot of doing.

I wondered if that was because I hadn't

sucked my reeds long enough, or what. But

whatever, I couldn't manage to play the

little song my teacher was playing, and
after almost an hour I began to get the
feeling that my learning to play the oboe
just wasn't going to happen.

But Dhat Turka wasn't discouraged. Not at
that point.

"All differences between people are
illusory," he said. "A Sikh man knows
that. I am no 'better' than you at playing
the oboe; we just are making different
sounds right now. Everyone everywhere is
equal. Here is what Sikh scripture says:
'I see no stranger. I see no enemy. I
look upon all with good will.'

"I believe, for instance," he added, "that

over time, you will teach me as much about the oboe as I teach you."

Though initially dubious, I sort of liked the sound of that, and the idea that I, a ten-year-old, was equal to all the grown-ups out there who acted superior to me, including my parents. Dhat Yurka told me that Sikhism's holy book, the Adi Granth, didn't tell a person what to do or not to do. He said that, instead, the Adi Granth was "a bouquet of poetic songs."

"Including, probably, the one we're playing here," he said. "Next time I come I'll give you a demonstration of the power of this particular song."

And sure enough, next time he brought with him a sizeable wicker basket with a lid on it. He set the basket on the kitchen floor.

"Inside this basket," he told me, "is our brother the snake. Watch how I please him with our song."

With that, he took out his oboe, removed the lid from the basket, and started to play:
"No, they don't wear pants in the southern part of France."

The words went through my head as he played the simple melody, over and over. And as he played, the hooded head of a sizeable snake came up from the darkness inside the basket. It was the head of a king cobra; I knew that from our snake studies, and that it was one of the deadliest poisonous snakes.

But this one seemed completely charmed by the little song. Its eyes never left my teacher's oboe, and its head moved rhythmically back and forth.

When Dhat finally stopped playing, the snake dropped back into the dark of the basket, the lid of which Dhat hastily put back on.

"You see?" he said.

"Yes," I replied. Then showing off:
"'Music has charms to soothe the savage
snake . . .', if I may take a small liberty
with old William Congreve." My mother had
had me memorize that line – with "breast"
in place of "snake" – in a class she taught
me called "Quotations that Make People Seem
More Intelligent and Well-read than They
Are." You should also know that once I
turned HS age, my curiosity impelled me to
seek out and read all the works those
Quotations came from. And I didn't think
much of Congreve's play, *The Mourning
Bride*, which contained the above quote in
Act I, Scene I.

A few weeks later, for my final exam in
Dhat's oboe class, he brought back the

snake in the basket, accompanied by his girlfriend, Phati - pronounced pretty much like "Patty", of course.

I played the "don't wear pants" song for the cobra, but my reed-control was a little off when I hit "southern" the second time, and the snake struck at the oboe, knocking it out of my hands. Phati quickly grabbed a paper towel and wiped the venom off the instrument before it could penetrate the finish. She told me that if the cobra had hit me instead of the horn, she would have made an x on the wound with a steak knife, and then sucked the poison out, but she didn't have to do that for my oboe. It'd "probably" be all right, she said.

Dhat tried to give me a C- in the class,
but my mother factored in all the time and
effort I put in sucking and practicing and
changed my grade to an A. This is, let me
assure you, the only example of grade
inflation on my transcript.

I chose to give up playing the oboe after
the snake incident, but I was determined to
seek out and enjoy my own "bouquet of
poetic songs." And so began my love affair
with opera, and later with the work of
Beethoven and most of the various Bachs.
(I was drawn to their enunciated
'h's',perhaps?) And to them I added good
helpings of jazz (Bessie, Louis, Duke, as
well as Miles and Bird and Monk), some
seminal folk (Huddy, Woody et al) and such

rock'n roll as I believed would stand the test of time.

Yes, My mother introduced me to "serious music", but I'm the one, I think, who made it a bosom friend.

Dean Dorman

1134 Honeysuckle Court   South Riddle, MA

Dear Tapi,

Uncross those fingers right away! Bury those doubts and "maybes" in a bucket of *blancmange* (instead of cherries jubilee or any other sweet high-calorie dessert). I've very much enjoyed your first five chapters.

I love it that you've given us both the before (as it was) and after (as it is) versions of yourself to chew on and enjoy. And I'm impressed at the way the emerging portrait of Tapioca Strangeways includes many of the lineaments which we in the Admissions Office look for (and admire) in an applicant. We hope to have a student body that is cut from a variety of cloths, and you, quite clearly, are someone who combines a soft pashmina with a sturdy blue denim. Although you were frank to warn me that parts of what you write may be "improved by (your) imagination", what I've read so far gives off a fragrance of truth that's as unmistakable as that of Harris Tweed.

I gotta say, in short, that I like "the cut of your jib".

And that nautical phrase reminds me that I've been wondering if that photo of yourself you sent us was taken on the shore of beautiful Lake Champlain, perhaps at Burlington's North Beach. If it was, then obviously one can get a better tan in northern Vermont than I ever imagined. A number of us in Admissions have regularly flown our pale and weary, sun-starved bodies to various tropical locations once we've finished choosing "the best of the best". But never with results as good as yours! Don't be surprised if you see a guy wearing a Riddle baseball cap stretched out on your favorite stretch of sand, next summer. (Just kidding!)

Anyway - enough of this extrinsic chit-chat. Do keep those chapters coming. And be assured: the more I see of you, the merrier (I am).

All the best,

Dean

"Go Sphinxes"

Tapioca Strangeways

P.O. Box 138
Rising Gorge, VT

Dear Dean,

"WHOOSH . . .!" was more or less the sound of the monster sigh of relief that I allowed myself after reading your letter. Your approval didn't just make my day. It also inspired me to sit right down and go to work on two more chapters, which I'm now able to enclose. They both will help you to understand my feeling that who I am was put together with Riddle University in mind.

And because you commented on my tan a while back, and I happened to mention it near the end of Chapter 7, I thought I might as well send you another snapshot of me on a beach, though maybe this one isn't "file-worthy."

Upwards & onwards, thankfully & joyfully,

Tapi

My Admissions Essay

Chapters 6,7

My Admissions Essay - Chapter 6

<u>Where I'm From</u>

I'm pretty sure I heard somewhere that Riddle and its jealous imitators/ competitors - Harvard, Stanford et al - strive to have "geographical diversity" in their entering classes. So I hope I haven't given the impression that I only lived in a couple of different locations before ending up here in Vermont. I've lived in - and enjoyed - so many parts of the country that it's hard to say, with certainty, exactly where I'm from. In fact, it's perfectly possible that I could provide all the "geographical diversity" a

University needs in one attractive package (*kidding*!).

I've already told you about my early days in the Projects, in a Midwestern city that I forgot to name before. It was Chicago: "Stormy, husky, brawling,/City of the big shoulders." as Carl Sandburg so neatly put it. And I did explain that we moved from there all the way to Long Island (NY) because my father wanted me to see life as lived by people in a different socio-economic bracket. So you already know about my living in two very diverse places. But there's a lot more geography in my history.

Because you've seen the return address and

postmarks on my mailings, you also are aware I'm now domiciled in a setting that's very different from both Chicago and Long Island. If Mr. Webster went looking for a synonym for "small town", he couldn't do any better than "Rising Gorge, Vermont". Here, I have definitely experienced small town life, and the various advantages and disadvantages it affords. And I suppose there'll always be a part of me – my neighborliness, for instance – that I picked up from my time here in "the Gorge."

Want proof that this town is *really* small? Well, I think if I report a conversation I had recently with the owner of our one-room General Store/Post Office – with single gas pump – you'll have all the proof you need.

Storekeeper: Mornin', Tapi. You hear that crash last night?

Me: Unh-unh. A crash, There was a crash?

S'keep: A-yup. Light plane. Single engine job. They say it went down somewhere nearby. In this town, for sure.

Me: How the heck do they know it crashed around here?

S'keep: From the radio message they say the pilot sent as he was going down. He said he was directly over Rising Gorge.

Me: How the heck did he know that?

S'keep: He said he looked down and didn't see nothin'.

I think you'll agree a town can't get much smaller than that!

Now, in between Long Island and Rising

Gorge I lived in a bunch of other places

I'd like to tell you about. AT one point

we were based in Queens (NY), and while

there, I - a linguistic and attitudinal

chameleon if there ever was one - became, I

think, a recognizable "Noo Yawker." It

helped that we made frequent trips into

Manhattan.

To give you an example of my adaptation to

new surroundings, I'd like to put down what

I recall of another conversation I had, in

which I spoke the demanding, crunchy

language that I call Big Appletalk. I

realize me putting down conversations

doesn't really "prove" I lived anywhere, or

even that they ever took place. I mean, me

showing up somewhere in a T-shirt with the

Eiffel Tower on it wouldn't prove I was from France, and me saying "*Que pasa, maricon*?" wouldn't prove I lived in the Dominican. But your last letter seemed to approve of my "telling it like it was"; I can only keep doing that and hope you find what I have written credible.

So all that being said, here's the conversation, as best I can remember it. I had it with a waiter at a Deli on Sixth Avenue – you notice I don't say "Avenue of the Americas" – where my dad had taken me for lunch.

> <u>Waiter</u>: So what's yours, kiddo?
>
> <u>Me</u>: Well, I'd like a pastrami on rye, but I can't finish one of those regu- . . .

Waiter (interruptingly): One pastrami rye, right.

Me: No. Chill, willya? Allus I can finish is about a halfa one of those regular sizers, so what I want . . .

Waiter (cutting me off again): So I'll put the other half inna doggy bag and yuh can take it home wid yuh.

Me (whiningly): But we're goin to a show right after and then meeting my mom for dinner, and then we gotta catch a ride back home. I can't lug around a halfa sandwich all day long. How about this? How about you give me a Coke steada the other half and we call it even?

Waiter: Look, kid. The kitchen don't make no halfa pastrami sandwiches. With pastrami, it's one size fits all. Take it or leave it.

Me (stubbornly): You mean even if we pay the full sandwich price for half a pastrami sandwich and a Coke . . .

Waiter (turning to my father): I got other tables, mister. The kid want the sandwich or not?

Me: Nah! *Fuhgeddaboutit*! I hate this crummy place!

We moved out of Queens (NY) shortly after
that.

I'm also reminded of another food incident
that took place a bit after that last one.
We'd spent the night at a motel in north-
eastern Tennessee, on the way to our new
home in that part of the state, and we'd
stopped at a diner for breakfast. All
three of us sat at the counter, and my
mother, in the middle, ordered the same
meal for everyone: eggs over light with
ham, plus coffee for her and my dad, and
milk for me.

When the lady put my plate of food in front
of me, I couldn't help noticing that
someone has slopped what looked like Cream

of Wheat right next to the eggs and ham,

with the toast on the other side of it.

And I wasn't in the mood for hot cereal.

"Excuse me," I said to this counter person.

"I don't want any of this stuff" - jabbing

at the white mass with my fork - "and I

know she didn't order it" - jerking my head

toward my mother.

"Don't say 'stuff'; it's not polite," my

mother said. But she was drowned out by

the lady behind the counter.

"You don't want your *grits*, honey?" was her

contribution to my education. "They *come*

with the eggs and ham."

"My *what*" I asked.

"Your *grits*," she said, firmly. "What'd you think they was?"

"I thought it looked like Cream of Wheat," I told her.

"*Cream of Wheat*?" she yodeled. "Where you from, sweetheart? You don't know *grits* when you see 'em?"

"I guess not," I said, and turned to my mother. "Do I have to eat that stuff?" Pointing at it with my wrinkled nose that time.

"Don't say 'stuff'," she said again. "If

you don't want your . . .grits, just push
them off to one side." I could tell she'd
never had the word "grits" come out of her
mouth before, or the food, grits, go into
it.

So ended my introduction to Tennessee, the
land of the Gritseaters.

For one final piece of evidence that I've
lived in a lot of diverse places, I'd like
to offer my recollection of what was said
when the doctor who was giving me a
physical exam, soon after we moved to a
certain southwestern state, got ready to
test my reflexes by tapping my knees with
his little rubber-headed hammer.

MD: Gollee dawg! What's this? What happened to your knees?

Me: My knees? Nothing, really. They're fine.

MD (fingering them, curiously): But you've got these little-bitty ridges on them. They look and feel like calluses. Kind of like the ones I've seen on the back of a linebacker's neck, if his helmet don't fit right.

Me (laughing): Well, they *are* calluses. But these ones came from ocean surfing, back where I lived before. You kneel on your board when you're paddling out to pick up a wave, and after a while you get these calluses.

MD (shaking his head): Well, me – I'm a Sooner born and a Sooner bred, and the only waves I know about are the ones we make on Saturdays if we're down at Norman for a game. I helped make waves when I was there in school, and I still do to this day. And you know something else? We now have a University our football team can be proud of, just like our President said we would.

I was pretty sure when he said "our president" he hadn't meant George W. Bush. I doubt he'd ever been President of any university.

My Admissions Essay - Chapter 7

<u>Diversitwo</u>

If there was one thing that always got packed very carefully, whenever we were getting ready to move, it was the family photo album. Both my parents loved to leaf through its pages and tell me about different relatives and ancestors, some of whom were still alive when I was born.

But, from a Riddle point of view, the important thing about those albums was probably this: they bore witness to another type of diversity embodied by yrs. truly: the roots I have in a lot of different religio-racial gardens.

"Now here's another shot of my mom's father," my dad might say, pointing to a man standing straight and proud behind a chair that had a woman with a baby on it. Though he had a regular suit on, I thought the man looked like what I already knew he was, a genuine Native American.

"He was your great-grandfather, of course," my dad might add, "accent on 'great.' Running-Bear McGregor was a true-blue, certified American hero."

"When he left the reservation and joined the U.S. Army at the beginning of World War One," he might tell me - again - "he called himself 'R.B.' instead of Running-Bear, 'cause there were still idjits out there who looked down on people they called 'Indians.' After he came home, he met and married your great-grandmother. Her christened name was Mary Jo - that's her in the picture - but everybody called her 'MJ'. My mother said it was fate, her meeting and marrying a man who also used just two initials, 'stead of a real first name."

At that point I'd probably plead with him to tell me the story - again - of how RB McGregor got to be a war hero, and he'd happily oblige. From time to time, some details might change or some facts be added or subtracted, but the main elements of the story always were the same.

It began in the fourth year of the War on the day that Running-Bear's squad - or platoon or company, or whatever it was - up there on the front line, ran out of ammunition. But RB wasn't ready to stop fighting, so he calmly put down his useless gun, climbed out of the trench that he'd been in, crawled on his belly across No Man's Land, slipped through the German lines, and arrived in a little forest where the enemy had stockpiled a ton of ammunition, plus an ocean of fuel for all their trucks and tanks.

Once he'd sized up the situation, RB came up with a plan. Using his trusty Bowie knife, he fashioned a simple bow and arrows out of the local woods and then used his stone-chipping skills to make arrowheads. These, he fastened to the arrows with the dental floss he always had in his shirt pocket, flossing being something that for all his life he faithfully did after every meal. A pair of luckless songbirds provided the feathers for the arrows' other ends. His bootlaces, tied together, became his bowstring.

Thus armed, he proceeded to silently dispatch the German sentries who were guarding the supplies. Then, from close range, he lobbed his last two hand grenades onto the tanks of fuel and cases of ammunition - and ran for his life, praying the Great Spirit would protect him.

The shock waves from the exploding
ammunition knocked him to the ground, and
the heat from the inferno that the burning
fuel became singed the soles of his unlaced
boots. But he staggered to his feet, and
in the resulting mass confusion he was able
to locate the German General's HQ and march
that significant captive back to the
American lines at the point of a rifle he
"borrowed" from one of the dead German
sentries.

When his platoon - or whatever it was - got
re-supplied with ammunition, it came out of
the trenches and attacked and routed the
still freaked-out German Army, thus ending
World War One and causing RB McGregor to be

awarded all the medals they gave to national heroes.

I'm sure you can understand why I *loved* that story.

Other ancestors may not have been heroes, or part of such action-packed adventures, but I believe they still made interesting contributions to the family's history and my DNA. One such was Solomon Tannenbaum, my mother's grandfather - who insisted, though supposedly with a twinkle in his eyes, that the song 'O Tannenbaum' was written about one of his kinsmen - who came to this country from Germany, landing on Ellis Island just off New York City, thus

making him a genuine "immigrant." Once he
learned English, he started his own
business, a convenience store that he
opened at 8 in the morning and closed at 12
midnight. Though it provided a fine living
for his family, his 8/12 store never became
the first of a chain. My mother told me
that he died an unhappy man, convinced that
if he'd only opened and closed his place an
hour earlier, at seven and eleven, he would
have made a fortune.

Because Solomon married a Chinese Catholic
woman name Yan, their children weren't
officially Jewish, so I guess I'm not
either. But I like to think I've inherited
some entrepreneurial skills from old
Solomon as well as the industriousness and

academic competency — esp. in math and science — of Yan's people. And if anyone looks closely at my eyes, I think he or she will see that they resemble Tiger Woods's — not surprising considering that we both have similar forebears. And I'm pretty sure that *my* eyes may have contributed to my — lesser — athletic successes, too.

One final ancestor who's probably worth a good mention is Bertram Strangeways's wife Jasmine, my father's mother and hence my grandmother. Though her darker sister Jemima — my great-Aunt — gained a lot more notoriety as a result of her place in the nation's grocery aisles, my granny was known in the family for her beauty, her grace as a member of the Martha Graham dance company, and for making Phi Beta

Kappa at her Ivy League college. I may not

look African-American - though people often

comment on the rich smoothness of my tan- I

believe I could claim to be, based on this

relationship. But my feeling is I wouldn't

want to slight my Native-American, Jewish-

American or Chinese-American roots by

saying so, so I've made it a rule to just

check the box in front of "White", whenever

I'm asked for my ethnicity. The

Strangewayses who came before me certainly

were White Anglo-Saxon Protestants though,

like myself, friends to all manner of

hyphenated Americans.

Dean Dorman

1134 Honeysuckle Court   South Riddle, MA

Dear Tapi,

Thanks for another delightful pair of Admissions Essays. Your folder's getting nice and fat as, simultaneously, we continue to realize how nicely your well-roundedness fits the Riddle profile.

In Chapter 6 you made reference to the "credibility" question – which I'd touched on in my last letter – and your sensitivity to that issue impressed me. I have the feeling you wanted me to know when you were giving us the unvarnished truth and when your "facts" were a bit improved by your imagination. And I think I do (know, that is).

Your evidence to prove you've lived in many different places – those remembered and reported conversations – rang very true, I thought. With minimal verbosity, you offered your readers valuable insights into the style and substance of people you brushed up against in the course of moving to and through the states of . . . let's see if I recall them right . . . Illinois, New York, Tennessee, California, Oklahoma, and Vermont!! Working for Riddle Admissions, I've traveled extensively in the good old U.S. of A., and the words you reported as coming from different people's mouths rang true to this pair of ears. And though it's possible I flatter myself, I'd have to say I have close to perfect pitch, speech-wise.

On the other hand, your reporting on "events" that precipitated the end of the first World War and (particularly) your assertion that you're related to a historical "Aunt Jemima" did stretch my credulousness, delightedly, to the breaking point and beyond – as I'm sure you knew they would. There was a nifty tongue-in-cheek-ness in your clever chronicling. So – no harm, no foul. What shone through in that chapter was your calm – indeed, happy – acceptance of all nationalities, races and religions, which is, of course, exactly what Riddle does, too. An absence of discrimination is one of the cornerstones – and keystones – used in the foundation and construction of this great University.

Having just gotten home from my daily workout in the Strength and Conditioning Center at the Riddle Field House, I sat down to write this letter feeling the "glow" of good health with which I'm sure you are familiar – going by the witness of the photo you sent along with Chapter 7.

Though you haven't yet favored us (in your Essays) with an explanation of how you developed the "healthy body" that accommodates your demonstrably "healthy mind", your photo made it super-clear you're in fantastic shape! And of course I've had to wonder where it was taken. My assumption is that you know an out-of-the-way beach where one is free to implement one's own dress code. How wonderful! The photo, though certainly "file-worthy", is locked in a desk drawer here, while remaining, in my mind, a most welcome (and some would say persuasive) part of your application.

Sorry to go on at such length, but you gave me a lot to examine, appreciate, and respond to.

My very best,

Dean

PS It seemed to me that, in the interest of fairness, you ought to know what your Riddle pen pal looks like. So, inspired by your example, I enclose a regrettably less "natural" photo of me.

"Go Sphinxes"

Tapioca

Strangeways

P.O. Box 138
Rising Gorge, VT

Wow, Dean!

Am I impressed, or what? You are
some kind of *hunk*!! I knew you were
articulate and caring and free-wheeling,
but I had no idea you looked like that! I
wouldn't be at all surprised to learn
there's a Mrs. Dorman residing in
Honeysuckle Court. But regardless of that
possibility, I've got your photograph on
the bulletin board that's on the wall my
desk faces. So, as I write, I'm admiring
your six-pack and the rest of you. It
makes it a little hard to concentrate, but
I can live with that.

Before I get into my workout history and
athletic "accomplishments", there's the
development of another side of me I'd like
to tell you about. It's an even more
important side in my opinion and, I expect,
in Riddle's.

So here comes Chapter 8, from a dazzled,

Tapi

My Admissions Essay

Chapter 8

My Admissions Essay – Chapter 8

Character Analysis

First, a few things I found out while researching a paper for English class last year.

Once upon a time, up to about the 1950s, I think, the best schools – "prep", boarding, all boys, mostly in New England – were into "building character." They came right out and said that, in their catalogues. And the great-grandfathers of kids my age, provided they were rich, went to those schools and then, once their characters had been built to the point they were "sterling", they moved on to the "best" colleges. I think those were basically Harvard and Yale – Princeton being too much of a "country club". The characters of the girls they later married were built mostly at home, where they learned how to act like "ladies." Some also went away to a handful of girls' prep schools. They were often named "Miss Somebody's", and they tried to put a high shine on their students' lady-like-ness.

Gradually however, things changed; for several reasons, I think. One probably was that colleges realized those prep schools weren't a hundred percent successful in their character building efforts. Some prep school grads were seen to be ill-

mannered, lazy and dishonest, even as more
and more colleges became every bit as good
as the "best." Pretty soon, even Harvard
and Yale were fishing in the pools of
talented applicants which were found in
public high schools all over the country.
Colleges everywhere put stock in
accomplishments; kids' test scores were
matters of public record and could be
compared with other kids' test scores and
accomplishments. Because there was no way
to test for sterling character, it was more
or less assumed, in the absence of a
criminal record.

But once again the colleges probably
noticed something: that a number of the
accomplished, high-scoring kids they'd

accepted turned out to be . . .well, *jerks*
- more interested in having a good time
than in exhibiting intellectual curiosity
or contributing to the community in which
they found themselves. I have to think
that in this day and age Riddle would (once
again?) want to learn more about the
character of its applicants. And, for that
reason, I'd like to swing open the door to
where I keep my core beliefs and give you a
peek at one that's important to this
particular applicant, this Tapioca
Strangeways.

It was implanted by my mother, years ago.
She was looking up at me while on her hands
and knees, and next to that white porcelain
appliance in what I believe some Brits call

"the loo." That at times she assumed this

position professionally is neither here nor

there. The important thing(s) are the ten

wise words she spoke to me that day, words

I will never forget.

"There is no lady-like way to clean a

bathroom floor," she said.

And she had a lot more on her mind than

telling me about how to have a sweet-

smelling, reasonably germ-free john.

She wanted me to know that to be successful

at anything a person has to make an honest

commitment to doing it – that you can't cut

corners, or worry about appearances, or

insist on being cool, or dainty, if you're
going to do a decent job.

I've swallowed and digested what she said.
My life has already proved to be full of
bathroom floors that have demanded
attention from me. There's no "lady-like"
way to research and write a term paper,
read a Shakespeare play, practice yoga,
write encouraging letters to prisoners of
conscience, or knit hats and scarves and
mittens for immigrant children new to
Vermont winters. Riddle, I am into hands-
on, sweaty, all the way.

I guess that explains why I'm writing these
Admissions Essays, and putting myself, my
future, on the line.

Dean Dorman
1134 Honeysuckle Court   South Riddle, MA

Dear Tapi,

I just can't resist sending you an immediate and hearty "Bravo!", in reaction to <u>Character Analysis</u>, Chapter 8 of your self-actualized Admissions Essay.

Thanks (sic) to you, I now can't read any of the regular, Riddle-mandated Admissions Essays without imagining, super-imposed on it, a tile floor covered with filthy, damp and crumpled paper towels, as well as splatters caused by somebody's bad aim.

If I may add another, even more personal note: many (if not most) people with your kind of looks feel no need to be concerned about character. They figure that given the great hand Mother Nature's dealt them, they already have it made and can write their own tickets, their own dance cards. Encountering someone who's the exception to this rule has (further) warmed the heart of this Admissions Officer, who's now pleased to think of himself as much more than merely someone passing judgment on an application. Indeed, in my own (blue) eyes and hopefully in yours, I'm nothing more or less than Tapioca Strangeways's new friend. And no, there isn't any Mrs. Dorman. I've looked for one, but no luck so far.

Admiringly,

Dean

"Go Sphinxes"

Tapioca Strangeways

P.O. Box 138
Rising Gorge, VT

Dear Dean,

      I was really happy to get your last letter. To tell you the truth, I've been thinking of you as a friend for some time now – rather than just as a College Someone it was my job to impress. Before you sent me that picture awhile back, I'd been imagining what you might look like. And in this case, the real thing was even better than the imagined one – like sometimes the character you see in a movie looks better than when you imagined him or her when you read the book? If you know what I mean. I think I'm babbling.

Anyway, here are Chapters 9 and 10. I guess I forewarned you about 9, but I decided to throw 10 in at the last minute, in spite of my reluctance – see the Essay – to do so. As of now, I'm thinking that 10 will conclude my – not too long-winded, I hope – Admissions Essay.

Your Friend, for sure,
Tapi

My Admissions Essay

Chapters 9 and 10
(The End)

My Admissions Essay - Chapter 9

<u>Body Language</u>

My father certainly deserves some of the credit for the shape I'm in today - as well as for most of the "athletic" skills I learned at his "suggestion." But his motives weren't a hundred percent admirable, I think it's fair to say. Even fifty percent admirable would be a stretch.

Let me start with his main stated reason for my starting running regularly, before the age of ten.

"I need for you to have a good strong heart-lung system," he told me. "It's important that you're in tip-top shape,

so you can take care of me when I'm older.

To be sure you get into that kind of shape

we need to start you now."

"But if running's so good for a person, why

don't you just start running yourself?" I

asked him. "If you do, and get in great

shape yourself, then you won't need me to

take care of you."

"No, no, no – a person has to start young,"

he said. "It's like with tennis. All the

decent players you read about started when

they were your age, or even younger. Like

the Williams sisters – that Serena started

at the age of four. Their dad got them out

on a court when they weren't much taller

than a racquet, and look at them now! At

my age you don't get max benefit from

exercise - that's a proven fact."

He then went on to say that if he had to

he'd tie a rope around my waist and pull me

along behind his motorcycle. "Sort of like

the way that old guy Mandelbaum did to

Jerry Seinfeld."

I'd seen that episode on "Seinfeld" and

remembered how miserable Jerry'd looked,

being pulled behind that Mandelbaums' car,

but I still muttered that it wasn't fair to

make me do something I was probably going

to hate.

"You want to talk fair?" my father said.

"Haven't I taken care of you for almost ten years now? Seems to me it'd be only "*fair*" — he made that quotation marks sign with his fingers — "if you took care of me for a few years when I'm older. And besides, you're going to thank me for making you do this, later on. You'll be glad I made you get in good shape, for all sorts of reasons."

Well, it turned out he was right about that. I never have stopped running, and recently I even added some parts-specific exercises to my routine. I like the . . . *physique* my workouts have given me, I admit it. And from running I've also learned that, with perseverance, I can succeed at

other tasks that may be unpleasant and
difficult, at first.

The other "athletic" skills my father made
me practice are a bit of a different story.
But they, too, have had their usefulness.
And they certainly are examples of what
one's body can do, when given sufficient
practice.

Nowadays, I consider them to be just funny
little show-offy things I can do, on the
level of being able to take a quarter from
out behind someone's ear. But originally,
my father used them to win bets with people
he'd met, mostly in bars. For instance:

    -In my early teens, I learned to drive
     a Titleist a good two hundred yards,

using a Champagne bottle rather than
a golf club. When I last did that,
two years ago, it was on a runway
at the Rutland regional airport, a
location chosen by my father who
also won fifty bucks on my
achievement. He taught me this little
trick after he saw a film of the
golfer Lee Trevino doing it.
-I also can make at least twenty out
of twenty-five shots at the basket
from the free throw line, blindfolded.
I became a great free throw shooter
after my father got, off the Internet,
the thirty five - I think the number
was - different elements that, when
combined, result in a perfect, can't-
miss free throw - and passed them

along to me. "There's no reason not to make 'em all," he said.

–When it comes to tossing playing cards, one at a time, into a fedora hat, I may be the best in the world. If the hat is twelve feet away, or closer, and the air in the room is still, I almost never miss.

–On demand, I can say out loud, at full speed, flawlessly, the following tongue-twister, three times.

> "Theophilus Thistle, the successful thistle-sifter, while sifting a fistful of unsifted thistles, thrust three thousand thistles through the thick of his thumb."

It may seem that, with all the practicing my father made me do, I wouldn't have had time for schoolwork or the oboe, or any sort of social life. But I did. What I became was a very structured and

predictable individual. Except, perhaps,

in my social life. When relating to

someone, one-on-one, I'm pretty

improvisational, and a little wild.

My Admissions Essay - Chapter 10

<u>Broadening Outlooks Abroad</u>

There's one other life experience I had
that I think I ought to tell you about
before my essay's done. I'm a little
reluctant to do so, but here goes.

Two years ago, a man who'd founded an
interesting service gave a talk at our
school. His company is called *Ecce Mundi* -
which is "Behold the World" in Latin, I
think - and what it does is place kids
who'd like to take a year off from regular
schooling in various "programs" overseas,
on every continent including Antarctica, if
you can believe it.

The guy spoke convincingly about the benefits to be gained by living in a culture very different from our own — how much this "broadened one's outlook", which he said was invaluable as "globalization replaced parochialism" — or words to that effect. In most cases, his company's services cost a good deal of money, but he said that "generous financial aid" was available to interested and worthy students who qualified. All this interested and attracted me a lot. I've always aspired to have a really broad outlook.

He also said — and this, I can promise you, didn't attract me at all — that living and working in another country "really greased the old college admissions machine."

Riddle, the last thing I'd want you to suspect is that my motivation for getting involved with *Ecce Mundi* and telling you about the months I spent in Chornya is that despicable. It may be a fact that I grew a great deal and accomplished a lot in my time there, but most of all I'm humbled by and grateful for the experience of living and working with the Chornyans. College admissions was the farthest thing from my mind when I signed up to go and live in another part of the world, thousands of miles from home.

As you doubtless know, the Republic of Chornya is - like Georgia, Moldova, Chechnya, Kazakhstan etc - one of the independent states that came to be following the break-up of the Soviet Union.

It is, in fact, the smallest and poorest of

those states. Living in a country that is

landlocked, with no major river and only

one rail line passing through it, the

majority of the citizens of Chornya are no

better off than the Russian kulaks were

before the Revolution. Using outdated

machinery, they work the rocky soil,

planting mostly potatoes, turnips and

carrots while tending to their small brown

cows. The milk from these they turn into

yogurt, which they eat a lot of and believe

is responsible for their long - if

miserable - lives. They credit the

carrots for their - mostly - curly hair.

It seems that *Ecce Mundi* had gotten in

touch with – and checked out – an English-
speaking Chornyan name Oyeh Yezerí who was
pleased to offer free room and board to
older high school and college students from
the USA, if they would help the members of
his extended family "to learn more English
and think like Americans" as well as with
their efforts to develop sustainable agri-
culture – or whatever – in their country.
I guess what all this meant was Mr. Yezerí
was looking for farmhands with capitalist
tendencies who were fluent in Yank-speak –
and would also work for no pay. I figured
I could handle that assignment.

When, after a number of flights in smaller
and smaller planes, I came down in the
little airport outside of Ochi, the capital

of Chornya, I was met by Mr. Yezerí and two male members of his extended family who looked to be of college age.

Their greetings — "Wazzup, 'ho?" and "Wanna hoo-kup?" — inspired me to ask their uncle — or whatever he was — who taught them their colloquial English.

"Nice boy from Darmutt Collitch," Oye Yezerí told me. "Always crackin' jokes. But he don't like the food or somepin'. Stayed a week and he's outa here."

In my first week I realized the "or somepin'" could have been the everyday farm work, which went on for long hours and was physically challenging. But the food, mostly potato, turnip and carrot soup with heavy dark bread and followed by yogurt, took a lot of getting used to, too. As I ate, I could feel my outlook – but not my hips or waistline – broadening.

Evenings were given over to "English conversations" with a half dozen different "family members" at a time. The subjects of these, prescribed by Oyeh, were apt to be "What kind of house – or car, or job, or haircut – is best?", "What shortcuts are there for getting from poor to rich?", "Is it possible to avoid paying all taxes?", "Dressing for success – how you do it?" and so on.

I did my best to respond to their good-

natured questions and comments, while at
the same time correcting their English.
But what I had to wonder about was what
earthly use it would be for them to know
that BMWs and Mercedeses and Lexuses were
all great cars when the average Chornyan's
income was something like $63(US). It
seemed there was small likelihood they
would ever even *see* such a car.

But toward the end of the second month I
was there something happened that would
dramatically change the lives of all the
Yezerís. When using the pump that filled
the trough the cows drank out of, I took
the time to really taste the water.

Of course I'd sipped it before — in many cups of tea and bowls of soup — and I'd gulped big mouthfuls when I was thirsty after work. But I'd never paid close attention to the stuff, before.

And when I did, I realized that it was like no water I'd ever had in my mouth. Not that it had any flavor. But its very tastelessness, I realized, was uniquely satisfying and refreshing — even cleansing. It didn't only slake my thirst. Its incredible purity and unsurpassed wetness seemed to make me more alert, self-confident, and even . . . happy.

"O-M-G," I muttered. And the next day, sharing space on what looked like a condemned school bus with chickens, ducks, a pot-bellied pig and many too many aromatic Chornyans, I was on my way to Ochi with a cold quart of the local H20 in my backpack.

There, I had a piece of great good luck. At the small US consulate, I met a young officer names Seamus O'Rourke. I think his brother is some kind of writer. He'd applied for a posting to Ireland but had been sent to Chornya instead. Ever since he'd arrived, he'd been looking for a way to make this worth his while. When he sampled the product, he immediately plugged into what I had in mind to do.

"My college roommate, a Max Profitt, is a

hotshot risk management guy at Dreamon Brothers," he told me. "When I tell him about this idea of yours it'll prove to be just the sort of risk Viagra that makes him prick up his ears and reach for his checkbook. What he can do – *will* do, unless I miss my guess – is provide the necessary capital and expertise to get the project up and running. That's in exchange for a percentage of the profits, of course."

He smiled and picked a bit of lint off his blazer's lapel.

"For a much smaller bite off the top," he went on, "I can make sure there are no import-export problems, either at this

end or back in the States. Let me zip off
a fax to Max . . ." He giggled. " . . .
a fax to Max, that's a good one. And I'll
wager that in less than 48 hours we can
have a proposal drawn up that you can take
back to your Mister whatever-the-hell-his-
name-is and his family that'll have the lot
of them doing the national dance, the
gashotski, with you on their shoulders and
jelly glasses of turnip wine on their
heads."

"Just one thing," I said. "After you and
Mr. Profitt get your percents, will this
still be a good deal for the Yezerís?"

O'Rourke smiled at me. "You're damn right
it will. They'll be the local Rockefellers.

And nationally beloved for having created

hundreds of well-paying jobs. I'd never be

a party to any scheme that screwed the

Chornyans. After five years here, I've

gotten to love the ignorant bastards."

Well, it seems that O'Rourke is as good as

his word. He and Profitt moved fast. Red

tape was shredded into confetti, and before

I left Chornya, big trucks were beginning

to lumber onto the Yezerí property; they

contained the makings of a modern water

bottling plant. Profitt's "people",

bearing samples of what was to be known as

"ChorSIPnya Water" had already secured

orders for the stuff that would make it

"bigger than Perrier and Dasani combined",

they predicted, by its second year on the

market. Young people especially, they said, would "eat it up." (sic)

And now, this year, with the plant up and running, I got a postcard from Oyeh telling me he would soon be driving "a damnbig new youbet Mercedes!"

Dean Dorman
1134 Honeysuckle Court   South Riddle, MA

My dear Tapi,

Thanks for Chapter 9: impressive, charming, dimensional. Having seen – photographically – the "after" of your exercise program, I was interested to learn what it's consisted of. And you certainly have some unusual "athletic" skills! The last of them was the only one I even considered trying to duplicate, but so far I haven't been able to speed through "Theophilus Thistle" successfully, even once. This from a man who's always been said to have an agile tongue – one known for more than tasting food and phrasing compliments!

I'd say that Chapter 10 puts the icing on a delicious and digestible cake. No Riddle applicant (and no Riddle undergrad who took a year off) has had as fruitful an experience as you had. You were brave (and altruistic) to even go to Chornya, and what you accomplished and learned there is awesomely impressive. I can't wait to sample ChorSIPnya Water the first chance I get. And I can aleady imagine you, at 25, raking in one of those big bonuses at some investment bank and making a major gift to Riddle. Kidding – but only about that last. You won't need any hints from me to do the right thing!

At this point, our office has your school records: grades, various test scores, etc. The numbers are, to be frank, somewhat below the Riddle standard. But the ten chapters of your Admissions Essay (which I have here) do a pretty good job of offsetting those hints of academic insufficiency, I believe. So now, the only potential asset that still could be added to your folder is the outcome of the optional interview, and I think for the sake of your application we should set one up.

As a rule, interviews take place on campus and, in my experience, are apt to be hurried and rather sterile, if not painful, affairs. In the case of many applicants, the standard "hour" is hardly enough time to give the interviewer a sense of their value to the University community. So, my thought is this: seeing as we've already broken the bonds of the usual procedures (with respect to the Admissions Essay), why not go one step further and do your interview in a setting that would make it not just painless, but a lot of fun.

To that end, I'd like to reserve us a couple of rooms, for the weekend, at the Westin, in Boston. There, we could relax, go out and eat some decent meals, (no grits!) maybe listen to some music or take in a show – as well as have abundant time for questions and answers. All at my (Riddle's) expense, of course. In this way, your interview would become an in-depth, one-on-one experience that I'm betting would allow me to state, unequivocally, that you are someone who should definitely be offered admission to Riddle.

How does this sound to you?

Looking forward,

Dean

"Go Sphinxes"

Tapioca

Strangeways

Box 138
Rising Gorge, VT

Dear Dean,

Your suggestion was a bit of a
surprise - a humungous big surprise,
really. I'd been expecting to have an
interview right at Riddle, where I haven't
even been yet. I was looking forward to
seeing the campus in person, maybe going on
a tour led by some student I could ask
questions to, someone who was sort of on
the same level as me. I figured I might
even get to meet that "Director" of
admissions you mentioned a while back, Dr.
Gladstone Bragg. It wouldn't hurt to have
a guy like him in my corner, if it ever
came to a vote on whether I was admitted or
not, would it?

One problem I have with your idea is that
getting to Boston from Rising Gorge if you
don't have a car, which I don't, involves
taking the bus - or, actually, two
different busses because you have to change
at White Creek. And the bus isn't free. I
haven't told you this before because I
didn't want to do a "Poor little me", but

both my parents are on disability now, and
I've been helping out at a local dairy farm
so I can bring home a little extra money to
help pay for the necessities like
groceries, the electric, and propane to
heat the house, all of which are sky high
these days.

But – and this is one huge BUT – meeting
and really getting to know someone who has
come to *personify* Riddle in my mind would
be about the biggest treat I could think
of. So what I'll do is find a weekend job
that'll at least pay for a one-way ticket
to Beantown on the Vermont Transit. I can
always hitchhike back, if need be.

So how about any weekend after this next
one?

Excitedly,

Tapi

Dean Dorman
1134 Honeysuckle Court   South Riddle, MA

My dear Tapi,

I definitely hear you when you say you're looking forward to seeing the campus, going on a tour, meeting one or more of the great kids who are already Sphinxes, maybe even saying "Howdy" (and more) to Dr. Bragg.

I'm sure all of that can be arranged before long.

A big reason I wanted you to have the kind of interview I suggested was, I must admit, because I believe you should be rewarded for all the time and effort you've put into applying to Riddle. That magnificent Admissions Essay of yours will go down in our office's history, I suspect. It will become the standard against which all other applicants' eagerness to be admitted will be measured. Giving you a weekend of "fun" was the prize that came to mind when I wondered what we could do for you.

I'm humbled to think that I "personify" Riddle for you. You're too kind. In my mind, I'm just a guy – a guy not a whole lot older than you – who's had a blast getting to know you, and value you, thanks to the terrific kind of person that you've shown me that you are, partly as a result of the extraordinary life you've had.

Truthfully, my heart beat faster and a lump came to my throat when I learned how you've stepped up and contributed financially to your family's welfare. I'm plain delighted to enclose with this note a prepaid round-trip bus ticket between Rising Gorge and Boston.

Weekend after next would be great for me! Do we have a date?

Your friend, and more,

Dean

"Go Sphinxes"

Tapioca
Strangeways

P.O. Box 138
Rising Gorge, VT

Dear Dean,

Thanks a lot for the bus tickets!
Now I'm really up for having a great time —
with you — in Boston, which I hear some
people call "the hub of the universe."
Because we're mostly Red Sox fans up here
in "the Gorge", I ought to fit right in!

I just have one last question. Seeing as
an interview is only "optional", and that
Riddle has "rolling admissions", and you
said that I've submitted everything that's
required to make my application complete
and I haven't heard anything official from
Dr. Bragg, I'm wondering how my chances of
getting in are really looking, right now.
Is there a problem I don't know about?

Curiously,

Tapi

Dean Dorman
1134 Honeysuckle Court   South Riddle, MA

Dear Tapi,

    No, there's no problem whatsoever. It just takes time for an application to roll through the proper channels. I had a nice talk with Dr. Bragg about you, in which I tried to paper over his concerns about your scores. Once I add to your folder what I'm sure will be my glowing report on your interview, you should get "the word" very shortly.

    Having gotten to know you on paper, I'm now looking forward to seeing you in the flesh! I'm sure that when you get to Boston you'll be "accepted" warmly everywhere you go.

    Excitedly,

Dean

"Go Sphinxes"

Mr. Dean Dorman
Admissions Dept.
Riddle University
Riddle, MA

P.O. Box 138
Rising Gorge, VT

Dear Mr. Dorman,

    After talking to my daughter Tapioca, I looked up "rolling admissions" for myself in the Riddle catalogue. And what I saw made it crystal clear to me that you people have to have made a decision on her application. How come she hasn't heard? Is what's in your catalog just a bunch of bullhocky, or what?

    Yours truly,

Cecil Strangeway

ps It happens I've studied to be a paralegal, so I know what words mean.

Dean Dorman
1134 Honeysuckle Court   South Riddle, MA

Tapi –

   Can't you get your dad to cool his jets? This is our busiest time of year, and all of us in Admissions are working flat out. You will hear, officially, the week after our interview. No promises, but your application would benefit from that little extra boost a favorable report on the interview could provide. Fingers crossed.

Hastily,

Dean

"Go Sphinxes"

Tapioca
Strangeways

P.O. Box 138
Rising Gorge, VT

Dear Dean,

I've got some kind of distressing news. My father snuck into my room when I was at work yesterday. He went all through my desk and found all your letters to me, which I'd wanted to save, as well as the bus tickets you sent. And he had some kind of fit! Here's what he said I should tell you, and I quote:

> "If this guy Dorman wants to keep his job and stay out of jail for attempting to transport a minor across state lines for immoral purposes, he'll make sure you get a fat envelope from Riddle Admissions toot sweet. Meaning by *return mail!*"

I'm really sorry about this. But there's no reasoning with my dad when he gets in one of his moods.

Regretfully,

Tapi

RIDDLE UNIVERSITY

Office of Admissions   Riddle University   Riddle, MA

Tapioca Strangeways
P.O. Box 138
Rising Gorge, VT

Dear Tapioca Strangeways,

Congratulations!

We have carefully reviewed your application and are delighted to offer you a place in the Riddle class of 2013.

If you intend to enroll, simply fill out . . .

Very truly yours,

Gladstone Bragg, PhD
Director of Admissions

"Go Sphinxes"

P.O. Box 138
Rising Gorge, VT

Dear Mr. Dorman,

I just wanted to let you know my daughter Tapioca gave me those bus tickets you were kind enough to send her, and I used them to give myself a delightful, fun time in Boston. That generosity and thoughtfulness is just typical of Tapi. Ever since her father died three years ago, she's taken every opportunity to do little extra somethings for her Mom.

I was thrilled she was admitted to Riddle, and I'm sure she'll do a good job there. I think she plans to major in English and thereby further her skills in Creative Writing. Thanks so much for your interest in her.

Yours Sincerely,

Melba Strangeways

About The Author

Julian F. Thompson is the author of the contemporary classic *The Grounding of Group 6* as well as seventeen other novels for young adults, many of which appeared on Best Books lists. He has worked with teens in settings as varied as summer camps and a state reformatory, but mostly as a teacher. In the 1970s he founded and directed an alternative high school. At present, he lives with his wife, the artist Polly Thompson, in Vermont.

www.ingramcontent.com/pod-product-compliance
Lightning Source LLC
Chambersburg PA
CBHW080833250626
47160CB00008B/2915